Hannah's TWO HOMES

Life in a "blended" family - a 5 year old's perspective

Melodie Tegay

This book is dedicated to all the children in blended families and to those parents who are committed to always providing them with a "safe place to fall."
~~ Dr. Phil Mc Graw – Families First~~

Printed in the United States of America
ISBN 978-1-64133-474-7 (sc)
ISBN 978-1-64133-475-4 (hc)
ISBN 978-1-64133-473-0 (e)

Library of Congress Control Number: 2018941902

Juvenile Fiction
18.05.11

AuthorCentrix
25220 Hancock Ave #300,
Murrieta, CA 92562

www.authorcentrix.com

AuthorCentrix

Hi, my name is Hannah!

I am five years old.

Mommy and Daddy don't live together-

so I live part-time with each of them.

At Mommy's house, I have my own room.

At Daddy's house, I have my own room too!

At Mommy's house, I have an extra daddy . . .

'cause Mommy is married to him now.

At Daddy's house, I have an extra mommy,

'cause Daddy is married to her now.

At Mommy's house, I have a little brother.

I will catch him so he doesn't get hurt.

At Daddy's house, I have a NEW baby sister!

At Daddy's house,

I have a younger brother too.

We have fun playing together . . .

But sometimes he teases me!

At Mommy's house, I have a dog and a cat.

At Daddy's house, I only have goldfish,

'cause Daddy is allergic.

At Mommy's house we celebrate Christmas.
We trim the Christmas tree.

I get LOTS of presents!

At Daddy's house, we celebrate Chanukah. Daddy lights the Menorah while we play the Dreidle Game.

I get LOTS of presents!

At Mommy's house, we celebrate Easter.

I look for Easter eggs and get chocolate bunnies in my basket!

**At Daddy's house, we celebrate Passover.
We have a special dinner called a Seder.**

**A piece of matzo is hidden and whoever
finds it gets some money as a reward!**

Sometimes, we celebrate special

occasions ALL TOGETHER!

It's really fun when BOTH my families

come to my birthday party!

Sometimes when I am at Mommy's house, I get a little sad because I miss my "Daddy family" . . .

and I wonder what they are doing when I am not there.

Sometimes when I am at Daddy's house, I get a little sad because I miss my "Mommy family' . . .

and I wonder what they are doing without me.

But most of the time, I am happy because I am part of the two best families in the whole wide world, and ALL the time . . . no matter where I am . . .

I KNOW I AM LOVED!

CPSIA information can be obtained
at www.ICGtesting.com
Printed in the USA
BVHW02s1824220818
525327BV00022B/263/P